Acknowledgement

Writing this book has been a pleasure and a blessing to me and I hope my readers. " The Red Clay Princess" has taken me on an adventure to a far away country to see, feel, and experience the journey of Mor-gan as a child growing up in Zimbabwe and her determination to follow her dreams in America.

I am deeply grateful to her for allowing us a glimpse into her past and to share the wonderful transformation to America. I am sure that she would thank her parents, friends, her community, and most importantly her ancestors whom she relied on for strength, guidance, and support.

To my family, the foundation of my strength and inspiration. Thank you for standing by me, understanding the demands of the creative process, and offering unwavering support. Your belief in me and your love have been my guiding lights throughout this endeavor.

The Readers: I extend my deepest gratitude to all the readers who will embark on this literary adventure. Your curiosity and openness to explore new narratives make the world of literature a wondrous place. It is my sincerest hope that my stories touch your hearts and leave a positive impact on your lives.

With a heart full of gratitude and appreciation, I thank each and every one of you for being a part of this book's creation and for supporting me as an author.

Sincerely,

Donald C Robertson Sr.

Dedication

To Morgan —

A woman shaped by red soil and resilience.
You grew up in the heart of struggle, where war and hardship marked
every day, yet you chose faith over fear, service over silence. In Zimbabwe, you gave your hands to the sick, your heart to the poor, and
your spirit to the healing of your people.

When you left, you carried that same fire across oceans. In America,
you kept working, kept giving, kept believing — living proof that no
matter where you are, purpose doesn't fade, and roots run deep.

This book is for you, and for every women who learns early that
strength is internal, isn't loud nor fierce, but it overcomes fear, it's
steady, and it serves.

Red Clay Princess:
A Child's Journey from War-Torn Zimbabwe to America"

The Palatial Home in Harare

Morgan was a beautiful ebony-skinned girl, with black hair, and captivating brown eyes. She was born into a life of luxury in Harare, Zimbabwe's capital city. Her father, Neville, owned a successful import-export business dealing in tobacco and precious minerals, while her mother, Grace, came from a family long associated with high-level government advisers and influential entrepreneurs.

Their estate sprawled over manicured gardens dotted with flowering jacaranda trees. In the morning, Morgan's window framed a brilliant purple haze that stretched toward the horizon.

Servants and handlers kept the estate immaculate and attended to the family's needs. Morgan's bedroom overflowed with the finest toys—porcelain dolls in embroidered dresses, intricate model cars, and even a miniature piano.

Yet, despite these lavish trappings, Morgan found her greatest joy outside playing in the sand and rich red clay. It made her feel at peace and close to mother earth. The garden's red clay stained her knees and fingernails as she molded the wet earth into little figures or simply squelched it between her toes, delighting in the sensation

Her parents occasionally disapproved, wondering why their daughter would pre-
fer dirt to dolls, but they indulged her curiosity. They saw that beneath her care-
free grin lay a budding spirit of exploration—one that would come to define
Morgan's life in ways they could not yet imagine.

A Carefree Youth

The Sabi (Save) and Runde Rivers played a significant role in Morgan's early years. On weekends, the family would pack a generous picnic of roasted maize, spiced chicken, and fresh fruit, then drive out into the bush. Where morgan would see the wild animals in their natural habitats, babies animals running behind their mothers and some animals out to hunt for food to feed their families.

The roads, sometimes paved but often dusty, led them through vast landscapes of tall grass and baobab trees. Morgan loved these outings—her mother's laughter mixing with the chatter of the servants who accompanied them, the swirl of the river's current reflecting the sun like shards of glass.

In these moments, Morgan felt free, blissfully unaware of the growing tensions within her country. While newspapers hinted at political strife, the warm Zimbabwean sun and the gentle lull of her parents' conversation shielded her from the harsher realities. Morgan's world comprised laughter, discovery, and family bonds.

An added layer to her upbringing was linguistic diversity. Morgan's parents frequently traveled for business, often accompanied by her so she could learn firsthand about the nation's people and commerce. Between meetings, Morgan played with local children, picking up phrases in both Ndebele and Shona. This linguistic gift would later broaden her worldview, though she had yet to realize its profound importance.

The Religious Mosaic

Morgan's family was staunchly Protestant. Every Sunday, they attended a grand colonial-era church, with tall steeples and stained-glass windows depicting biblical scenes. Morgan, adorned in her best frock, listened to sermons that emphasized faith, community, and service. Her parents would linger after the service, speaking with the pastor and friends about community events or upcoming charity drives

Beyond their Protestant circle, Morgan encountered the vibrant tapestry of religions in Zimbabwe. Some of her school friends were Catholic or Anglican, and she learned about Methodist congregations through family acquaintances. Even more fascinating were the indigenous spiritual beliefs she heard about from her language tutors or the servants who worked in the estate. They spoke reverently of Mwari in Shona culture or uMlimu in Ndebele tradition—deities that connected the physical world to the ancestors watching over the living.

In hushed tones, she also heard about the darker side of the spiritual realm: the evil spirits called Ngizo, often invoked by witches or malevolent individuals seeking harm. As a child, Morgan found these stories both frightening and mesmerizing. Though her own faith was rooted in Christianity, she could not help but feel a quiet awe at the idea of ancestors forming an invisible community around the living—a notion of eternal connection that left a lasting impression on her young mind.

Shadows of a Nation in Turmoil

As Morgan grew older, whispers of political uncertainty filtered into her once-sheltered world. In the late 1960s, Rhodesia—what is now Zimbabwe—declared its Unilateral Declaration of Independence (UDI) from Britain. While Morgan was initially too young to grasp the full significance, the reverberations became increasingly apparent. International sanctions and diplomatic isolation put strain on an economy heavily dependent on trade.

13

Drought struck the countryside, and tensions mounted as white emigrants arrived or left amid the uncertainty, disrupting both land and labor. Farmers lost crops; businesses lost clients. Even Morgan's father, once confident in his flourishing enterprise, found contracts suddenly canceled and overseas clients hesitant. Subtle changes began at home: a reduction in the household staff, fewer elaborate dinner parties, and conversations laden with cautious undertones.

Morgan sensed these shifts but lacked the historical context to fully understand. She only knew that her parents were more serious, more anxious. The gilded cage was still intact, but its bars were starting to show wear.

A Troubled Society

Traveling with her parents allowed Morgan to witness the stark disparities between her life and the reality of most Zimbabweans. She saw communities with inadequate schools, medical clinics lacking basic supplies, and stories of underfunded health services and neglected education for the black majority were no longer just rumors. They were a visible truth.

On these trips, Morgan made small but poignant observations. She watched children fetch water from distant wells under the hot sun, their sandals threadbare. She spoke with villagers who, despite their hardships, greeted her with warm smiles and offers of roasted peanuts or freshly cut sugarcane. Their kindness contrasted with their hardships—a realization that stirred compassion in Morgan's heart.

One pivotal moment came when she witnessed an ailing grandmother turned away from a local clinic due to lack of medicine. The woman's granddaughter pleaded for help, tears streaming down her face. Morgan, shaken, began to question why some people prospered while others suffered needlessly. Seeds of discontent and empathy began to grow in her mind, foreshadowing a more profound awakening. Morgan remembered the stories of the evil spirits called Ngizo, often invoked by witches or malevolent individuals seeking harm. Ngizo had come and invaded the souls of the white –minority government.

Conflict Erupts

By the early 1970s, simmering tensions reached a boiling point. Various liberation movements, fueled by decades of disenfranchisement, rose to challenge the white-minority government. Sporadic violence and guerrilla warfare gave way to widespread fear. Curfews were imposed in certain areas, and stories circulated of bombings or skirmishes between rebels and government forces. Morgan was at first full of fear, but then she remembered the stories by the elders, that deities that connected the physical world to the ancestors watching over the living. The idea of ancestors forming an invisible community around the living—a notion of eternal connection that left a lasting impression on her young mind.

As Morgan grew older daily life in Harare changed. Police checkpoints appeared on roads once familiar and free. Nighttime gatherings became rarities; the hush of evening was no longer comforting but tense. Morgan's friends whispered about relatives joining the struggle or disappearing in the middle of the night. For Morgan, the realization came hard and fast: her beloved homeland was not only a paradise of rivers and gardens. She called upon her faith and teachings to transformed her fear into bravery and positive actions.

Her homeland was in turmoil but it was also a battleground for justice, education, power, and survival. No longer sheltered by childhood innocence, she felt compelled to acknowledge the suffering and yearning for change that permeated her country. She became quieter at home, often lost in thought. With each passing day, Morgan's determination to help in whatever way she could grew stronger.

Stepping into the World

The Turning Point

In her late teens, Morgan gravitated toward volunteer work through her church. She visited overcrowded townships, lending a hand in makeshift clinics and helping distribute food. Her parents, torn between pride and fear, watched nervously. Though they admired her willingness to serve, they worried about the dangers lurking in the city's peripheral neighborhoods, where protests and police raids were common.

One afternoon, during a particularly tense handout of mealie-meal (cornmeal), a confrontation erupted between the police and a group of protestors. It was Ngizo spirit attacking the community and causing harm and suffering. Panicked, Morgan dropped the bag she was carrying in fear and cried. . Tear gas stung her eyes; the cacophony of shouts and gunshots rang in her ears. This was the defining moment that Morgan said No more will I be afraid of Ngizo I will call upon IMwari and uMlimut the good ancestorial spirts to protect me and the people of the community. She realized her commitment to aiding the vulnerable outweighed her own fears. Morgan felt that if more people hd faith and prayed together that the spirits would come to protect their community, but the people were afraid and had forgotten the teachings of the elders.

At home that evening, her parents expressed both relief that she was unharmed and concern that she was venturing too far into the epicenter of unrest. But Morgan's resolve was sealed—she could no longer stand by, passive and privileged, while her people suffered.

Shattered Illusions

The economy deteriorated. Harare's once-bustling markets now showed signs of scarcity. Grocery stores began rationing, and lines formed outside banks that were short on currency. Morgan's father had to sell off parts of their estate to maintain financial stability. Several beloved family heirlooms, including antique furniture and artwork, disappeared to help pay bills.

Morgan witnessed the pain etched on her parents' faces as they came to terms with their vanishing fortune. The estate that once held lavish parties now seemed hollow, the staff reduced to a faithful few. For the first time, Morgan felt intimately connected to the struggle unfolding across Zimbabwe. Though her hardships still paled compared to those of the poorest citizens, the erosion of her family's wealth was a jarring reminder that no one was truly safe from the turmoil.

In the midst of this uncertainty, Morgan found that her faith and empathy offered some solace. She continued volunteering, offering hope where she could. Yet, she was increasingly convinced that Zimbabwe's problems would require profound change—something she was unsure her country could achieve under present circumstances.

The Decision to Leave

Friends and acquaintances began leaving Zimbabwe, departing for the United Kingdom, South Africa, or the United States. They cited safety, education, or job security as reasons, though all carried a sense of heartbreak at abandoning their homeland. Morgan wrestled with the choice. She felt an obligation to remain, but also recognized that she could accomplish more if she left to gain advanced education and resources.

She took a hand full of Zimbabwe's rich red soil with her in a cloth and held it close to her heart as she vowed never to forget her family, her people, and her country she knew as a child in the palatial home where she played in the garden as a child.

It made her feel warm and allowed her to maintain her connection with the people as she began her new life in America.

Her parents, once resistant to Morgan leaving Zimbabwe, the idea, eventually supported her. If she thrived elsewhere, perhaps she could send aid back home, or even return one day better prepared to help rebuild.

The day Morgan boarded the plane was bittersweet. She looked out at the fading skyline of Harare and imagined the jacaranda trees she had loved so dearly. She silently promised that she would not forget the lessons Zimbabwe had taught her—the beauty, resilience, and heartbreak etched into its soul.

A New Life in America

Adjusting to the American Dream

.Morgan arrived in the United States with hope, fear, and a single suitcase. St. Louis, Missouri, was her new home—a place with its own storied history of racial tensions and civil rights struggles. Although she was fluent in several languages and her English was very polished, she quickly learned that American language and cultural norms could be confusing. The people here were from many different lands and spoke many languages and cultures.

Her first months were spent navigating her new home—setting up a bank account, applying for nursing programs, and finding modest housing. She had saved what she could, supported by her parents' last vestiges of wealth and the help of distant relatives who had emigrated to America years before.

The most shocking realization came when she encountered subtle racism: a land-
lord who hesitated to rent to her, a passing stranger's suspicious glances. These
moments echoed the deep-seated inequalities she had witnessed in Zimbabwe,
reminding her that no country was without prejudice. Again Ngizo hate had
showed itself and left its effect on some of the people in America.

Morgan called upon her faith which was strong, and prayed to her ancestors by
name calling them to rise up to protect her in this new land she was now living.
She asked that her ancestors to bless her community here and at home that they
would find strength, peace, and success.

The attempts to harm or frighten her did not succeed, in fact she took these nega-
tive feelings and fears as she had done in Zimbabwe and used them to give her
courage, strength, and increased dedication to succeed.

Challenges and Triumphs

Determined to make the most of her opportunity, Morgan threw herself into her nursing studies. Long hours of coursework, clinical rotations, and part-time jobs left her exhausted but fulfilled. In the process, she created a support system, a new community comprised of friends, coworkers, and teachers to keep her focused and undistracted from her goals. Morgan welcomed fellow nursing students from various backgrounds, Mary from England, Sherry from the United Kingdon, Tonya from the Bronx, and Shesi from Japan, shared her sense of purpose. They formed study groups, celebrated each other's successes, and commiserated over difficult exams.

Over time, Morgan's expertise grew, and she earned the respect of her professors and peers. During a clinical placement at an underfunded community clinic, she felt that old spark of empathy ignite once more. Many of the patients were immigrants or low-income families, and their struggles mirrored those she had seen back home. In helping them, Morgan felt closer to Zimbabwe—she was, in essence, continuing the mission she had begun there. She never forgot about here homeland and often called home to her parents and sent money and books for the people in her town to learn about democracy, other cultures, and the power of community faith...

A few years into her life in America, she met Daniel, a kindhearted pharmacist who volunteered at the same clinic. Daniel was a Baptist and form Mississippi a southern stat with some people who were similar to the white Europeans in Zimbabwe. He vowed to make a difference in America by making him self the best man that he good be and to giving back to his community.

They bonded over a shared passion for service, justice, and helping the less fortunate, eventually falling in love. Despite cultural differences, they found common ground in their faith and in their desire to build a meaningful life together.

Love, Family, and Purpose

Morgan and Daniel married in a small church ceremony, surrounded by friends and her maid of honor daughter Zire who was the ring girl. who had become like family. Her parents came to America for the wedding. They were so proud of Morgan and what see had accomplished with her life.

They thanked her for never forgetting about her family back in Zimbabwe and her countrymen which she sent money to the poor churches, books to the children, and messages of hope and faith that one day they too will achieve justice.

Not long after, she and Daniel were blessed with twin girls, that she named Grace and Thandi. Morgan could not wait to spread the red clay on their little feet so they too would know the soft warm earth of her homeland.

She began to remember her life in Zimbabwe as a free spirited child, curious and adventurous child stomping through the red clay in the garden. .As she grew became older she remembered how she had faced with the realities of the conflicts in her country and struggle of her countrymen.

This is where she decided to be a part of making things better by studying hard, and helping others.

She told her daughters that they too must be unafraid and fearless as they grow older, and look to be a service to others. Embrace changes in your lives because you never know where it will take you. Coming to America was scary but exciting and gave me your great father and you two wonder-

Balancing motherhood with a career in nursing was demanding, but Morgan thrived. She continued sending money back to Zimbabwe regularly, supporting extended families and donating to local charities that funded clinics, schools, and food programs.

Each month, she wrote letters to her parents, describing her life in America—the challenges, the joys, and the dreams she still harbored for Zimbabwe. She also passed on stories of freedom and opportunity to her children, emphasizing that their heritage came from a land of extraordinary beauty and resilience

Morgan would often whisper Shona or Ndebele phrases to her young ones, teaching them lullabies from her homeland. In doing so, she hoped to preserve a piece of Zimbabwe within them, ensuring they understood the significance of helping those in need—wherever they might be.

Legacy and Return

Reconnection and Reflection

Years passed. Political leadership changed in Zimbabwe, yet economic and social challenges persisted. Morgan observed these shifts from afar, monitoring the news with both hope and concern. She continued to send donations to medical clinics, corresponded with old friends, and watched as some improvements were made, while new problems arose. However small the progress the country was moving closer to democracy and self determination.

When her children were old enough to understand their roots, Morgan decided it was time to return for a visit. Organizing the trip took months of planning. She worried about how she would find her once-grand home and whether the city she loved so deeply had transformed beyond recognition.

.Her arrival in Harare was a mixture of nostalgia and heartbreak. The jacaranda trees still lined certain streets with purple splendor, but the infrastructure showed wear from years of neglect. Friends from her youth were now scattered—some had immigrated, some had remained and adapted, and some had passed away. Still, there were signs of hope: new businesses, community projects, and a generation unafraid to push for change.

Full Circle

At last, Morgan stepped through the rusted gates of her family estate. Overgrown vines tangled with broken cobblestones, and part of the main house had crumbled from years of disuse.

Yet she could still sense the lingering echoes of laughter, remember her childhood footprints in the red clay.

.Emotions flooded her: sorrow for what was lost, gratitude for what remained, and renewed determination to help revitalize her homeland. She reached out to neighbors and old family friends, learning about local initiatives—schools that needed supplies, women's cooperatives struggling to break into sustainable markets, and medical facilities desperate for resources.

Before she departed for the United States again, Morgan laid out a plan: connect American nonprofits with Zimbabwean communities, funnel donations and expertise, and eventually create a foundation that could empower grassroots projects. Morgan's faith and experiences in Zimbabwe had made her strong and fearless to overcome many challenges. Her time in America had given her an opportunity for a better education, to make many friends, contacts, and financial stability.

Now she would use those assets to uphold the promise she made to herself long ago: never to forget the people she left behind. So she started many groups, and charities in Zimbabwe while on her trip and continued to support them while back in America.

The day came for Morgan and her family to return to America. The people were so proud of her and vowed to continue the work she had started and supported over the years. As she boarded the plane she thought what a wonderful journey I have been on. Morgan waved goodbye to her friends and family as she boarded the plane feeling that she had come full circle and had truly   accomplished the teachings of her ancestors by supporting the people strengthen and protects the community.

The twins were excited and inspired from there adventures and would never forget their visit and the people of Zimbabwe. They would always be connected to the country and its people. They would return to Zimbabwe and continue to make a difference some day. Goodbye till then.

Goodbye!

About this book

Red Clay Princess is a powerful coming-of-age story rooted in resilience, heritage, and hope. Born into privilege in Zimbabwe, a young girl watches her country unravel into conflict and poverty. Despite the turmoil, she stands firm, drawing strength from the teachings of her elders and doing what she can to uplift those around her.

When she leaves for America in search of opportunity, she faces new struggles, but the voices of her ancestors guide her toward success. A deeply moving story of identity, perseverance, and homecoming, *Red Clay Princess* is a tribute to the power of remembering where you come from—and passing that legacy on.

ISBN: 9798283598529

Bound and printed in St. Charles Missouri